Floodgates of the Wonderworld

Floodgates of the Wonderworld

A *Moby-Dick* Pictorial

Celebrating the 150th Anniversary
of the Publication of Melville's Masterwork

Robert Del Tredici

The Kent State University Press · *Kent, Ohio, & London*

05 04 03 02 01   5 4 3 2 1

Designed and composed in Centaur by Will Underwood.

Printed by Everbest Printers, Ltd.

Library of Congress Cataloging-in-Publication Data

Del Tredici, Robert.

Floodgates of the Wonderworld : a Moby-Dick pictorial :
celebrating the 150th anniversary of Melville's masterwork
/ Robert Del Tredici.

Includes bibliographical references.

ISBN 0-87338-703-1 (alk. paper) ∞

1. Melville, Herman, 1819–1891. Moby-Dick—Illustrations.

I. Title.

PS2384.M62 D45 2001

813'.3—dc21

2001029209

British Library Cataloging-in-Publication data are available.

For Alain Renoir,
who launched me
and Beth Schultz,
who pulled me from the deep

Acknowledgments

This book was a long time coming. I thank Rex May for
having imparted to me in the 1950s the art of designing
punchy greeting cards and Father Bob Giguere in the
1960s for steering my pencil down metaphysical paths.
When I began in earnest on the Melville pen-and-inks,
Etel Adnan helped me keep the vision primal. My long-
tolerant mother, Helen, sheltered the drawings for thirty
years in the attic of our San Anselmo home. Bob Wallace
got me silk-screening again, and Jill Gidmark quickened
my Melvillean pulse. I'm grateful to Sandy Marovitz for
inspiring my publisher and to Henri Hadida for heading
up prepress production in the nick of time, connecting me
with Peter Griffin, who helped beyond the call to ready my
screen prints for the Hong Kong press. My wife, Setsumi,
held down the fort with Felix in the final year of printing.
Frank Stella doesn't know it, but he gave me a big boost,
as did Thomas Berry and Daniel Quinn. And I gratefully
invoke the spirit of my dear aunt, Martha Mood, the first
to bless the art impulse inside me.

Contents

The Seer & the Scene

Robert Del Tredici's Illustrations for Moby-Dick

ELIZABETH SCHULTZ

In light of the stunning diversity and number of illustrated editions, paintings, sculptures, environmental works, performance pieces, cartoons, advertisements, and films that have been created the world over in response to Herman Melville's *Moby-Dick* (1851) throughout the twentieth century, it is possible to assert that this novel has appealed to visual artists more so than any other American literary text. Among these *Moby-Dick*-inspired artists, Robert Del Tredici, with his portfolio of small pen-and-ink drawings (8½" x 11", 1964–65) and his twenty large silkscreens (22½" x 30", 1990–2001), provides a unique and dazzling visual interpretation of Melville's complex novel.[1]

Unlike those illustrators and painters committed to illuminating *Moby-Dick* through narrative and portraiture, Del Tredici focuses on the novel's "little lower layer[s]."[2] His focus, thus, is on *Moby-Dick*'s inner drama—its philosophical and psychological dimensions, especially as they are experienced and perceived by Ishmael, the novel's narrator—rather than on the novel's outer drama, which involves either the relationships among the characters or the pursuit of the White Whale. In giving visual embodiment to moments of concentrated abstract awareness in Melville's novel, Del Tredici's images counter Rockwell Kent's *Moby-Dick* illustrations, on the one hand,

1. The number of Del Tredici's *Moby-Dick*-related pen-and-ink drawings number at least eighty-five, forty-five of which are reproduced here. Of the twenty silkscreens in this volume, eleven of their images were derived from the small portfolio drawings and nine are new, and Del Tredici, who perceives *Moby-Dick* and his response to the novel as ever-open-ended, claims to have ten more large works "in the offing." Conversation with the author, Feb. 28, 2001.

2. Herman Melville, *Moby-Dick*, ed. Harrison Hayford, Hershel Parker, G. Thomas Tanselle (Chicago and Evanston: Northwestern UP and Newberry Library, 1988), 164. Subsequent references to this edition will appear in the text.

which from 1930 have helped to popularize *Moby-Dick* nationally and internationally, often through oversimplified allegories and portraiture, and Barry Moser's *Moby-Dick* illustrations, on the other hand, which from 1979 have become well known for their particularized and realistic representation of the novel's physical objects.

For Del Tredici, "the essence of this many-layered book" is "perception itself": "What takes the book outside the boundaries of the adventure epic genre and renders it timeless, to me, is the assiduous focusing on the ins and outs of the human psyche in its struggle to perceive reality. So it's not only a book about whales, it's also about illusions and obsession, seeing and blindness, and the tilt we put on things with our own motives that we may well be not aware of."[3] For him, *Moby-Dick* is "a book about being a see-er, a pair of wandering eyeballs and psyche-strings, acting and being acted upon, and savoring the uniquely briny flavor of the human condition."[4] As his images consistently reveal, Del Tredici recognizes that it is Ishmael's "wandering eye-balls and psyche-strings," his perceptions, that are at the heart of Melville's undertaking: "It was at once [Melville's] protean style with Ishmael's consciousness at the center of it that captured and held my attention—and made merely narrative, sailor-based, pictures seem, well, disappointing as they missed the metaphysical part of the epic, the part that Melville repeatedly

3. Robert Del Tredici, letter to author, Dec. 17, 1989.
4. Robert Del Tredici, letter to author, May 18, 1990.
5. Robert Del Tredici, letter to author, Nov. 6, 1989.

admonishes his readers to take cognizance of."[5] Del Tredici's pictures, which combine his own protean style with an Ishmaelian perspective, give visible embodiment to his impassioned conviction regarding *Moby-Dick*'s significant invisible dimensions. Quotations from the novel, only a few of which have been the explicit subject of other artists' work, are incorporated into the aesthetic design of each picture, anchoring them in the nuances, subtle and expansive, of Melville's language.

To project a vision of Melville's metaphysical, mystical, and psychological musings, Del Tredici uses bold and energetic lines and often fantastical images to lift his pictures out of the realm of social reality into the realm of perceived and felt reality. Whereas other artists, for example, have responded to Melville's scene of the tranced narrator in Chapter XXXV, "The Masthead," by depicting a realistic scene with a man gazing forth from the ship's masthead, Del Tredici depicts the ship itself "gently rolling" among circular cosmic shapes, swaying between galactic ribbons, evoking "the inscrutable tides of God" (159). His images may be of demons, as in his illustration of a muscular winged figure, singed by a smoking-breathing whale, for a passage from Chapter XCVI, "The Try-Works": "The smoke of the whale has an unspeakable, wild, Hindoo odor about it, such as may lurk in the vicinity of funeral parlors. It smells like the left wing of the day of judgment; it is an argument for the pit" (422). Or they may be of divinity, as in his illustration of a gigantic foot crushing dense nebulous organic matter for a passage from

Chapter XCIII, "The Castaway": "Carried down alive to wondrous depths, Pip saw God's foot upon the treadle of the loom, and spoke it; and therefore his shipmates called him mad" (414). Pip in this image appears as a minuscule form, tumbling helplessly toward the foot's grotesque massiveness. To illuminate Melville's testimonial that "Yes, as every one knows, meditation and water are wedded forever" (24), Del Tredici creates a simple, meditative dharma figure, who, in filling the picture's space, also appears to encompass the heavens and the earth.

Ishmael himself often appears in Del Tredici's pictures. He is represented diversely—as a bard strumming his lyre at sea in a cockle-shell; as a quizzical figure striding down cobblestone streets with multiple whales leading him on; as a necromancer pondering manuscripts illuminated with whales; as a man comfortably seated on whale's back in an overstuffed chair; as an individual who can swim with whales or look a whale in the eye. Reflecting his scholarly interest in the history of the comic book as well as his sensitivity to *Moby-Dick*'s multiple levels of humor, Del Tredici's renderings of Ishmael can be comically, even whimsically, appealing. In each depiction of the novel's narrator, Del Tredici presents him as minute: he is finite humanity confronting infinitudes; tiny man adrift in cosmic oceans. For example, his illumination of the opening lines from the first paragraph of Chapter XLIX, "The Hyena"—"There are certain queer times and occasions in this strange mixed affair we call life when a man takes this whole universe for a vast practical joke, though the wit thereof he but dimly discerns" (226)—places his small Ishmaelian figure alone in a boat in the picture's lower right-hand corner, while in the arched sky above him, like a bizarre and enigmatic constellation, looms a grimacing hyena head.

Reflecting what he identifies as Melville's protean or "kaleidoscopic style,"[6] Del Tredici's pictures do not follow any definitive narrative order, let alone *Moby-Dick*'s chronological order. They reveal *Moby-Dick* to be, as critic Andrew Delbanco testifies, "an outburst of a fluid consciousness in which ideas and persons appear and collide and form new combinations and sometimes drop away."[7] Despite their envisioning specific passages, his images, as individual drawings and prints, may be shuffled or arranged in any order. Del Tredici's kaleidoscopic sense of the novel's narrative is reinforced by the fact that the drawings appear on an assortment of colored paper, including forest green and magenta, gold and silver; for his silkscreens, he relies on multiple shimmering colors.[8] Several of his silkscreens are kaleidoscopes in themselves, exuberant in their swirling colors. For example, the photo offset print of Pip's apprehension of

6. Robert Del Tredici, letter to author, Nov. 6, 1989.

7. Andrew Delbanco, "Introduction," *Moby-Dick* (New York: Penguin Books USA, 1992), xvii.

8. Dismayed at the paucity of colors commercially available for silkscreen artists, Del Tredici uses a diversity of inks in his prints, many of which he mixes himself; these include woodstain, antiquing chemicals, powdered paints discovered on beachcombing expeditions, as well as a range of interference colors, in which mica flakes in several sizes are suspended in a clear medium.

"God's foot upon the treadle of the loom" is transformed through gorgeous overlays and juxtapositions of color, with Del Tredici thus extending his image well beyond the scope of the quotation by evoking Pip's comprehensive, chaotic, and oxymoronic vision of "joyous, heartless, every-juvenile eternities," of "the multitudinous, God-omnipresent, coral insects, that out of the firmament of waters heaved the colossal orbs" (414). By creating his illustrations for *Moby-Dick* in reference to vision rather than to the narrative's characters and coherence, Del Tredici takes his viewers, as Melville does his readers, off the page into explorations, terrifying and wondrous, beyond conventional spatial and psychic boundaries.

ELIZABETH SCHULTZ

Melville Cave Art, Modern Students

Robert Del Tredici's Primal Pen and Inks

JILL B. GIDMARK

I share my office on the East Bank of the University of Minnesota with a potent, fertile, exploding array of artwork by Robert Del Tredici: forty-one framed *Moby-Dick* pen-and-ink illustrations, nineteen matted black-and-white photographs, a large cross-hatched pen-and-ink landscape of rural Spain, and a two-sided, multifaceted painting entitled *The Left Wing of the Day of the Queen of the Happy Faces*. There are seven boxes of his *Moby-Dick* slides on my desk and a twelve-foot-long blueprint scroll of his poster-sized *Moby-Dick* images in a tube next to my computer. Published books by Del Tredici line my shelves: his interviews and photographs documenting the aftermath of the meltdown at Three Mile Island, the U.S. nuclear weapons complex, and the U.S. government's first serious attempts to clean up its radioactive H-bomb factories after the Cold War—along with his Concordia University *History of Animated Film Resource Book*. Del Tredici's multidisciplinary imagination arcs through my office space into my spirit with an energy that is wrenching, euphoric, forthright, startling, and strangely uplifting.

The trajectory of Del Tredici's oeuvre is uncannily akin to Melville's own spiritual development, especially as it expressed itself in *Moby-Dick*. Ishmael, the novel's wandering narrator-mariner and sole survivor of cosmic watery cataclysm, enables the reader to identify with the story, pulling us in in spite of, and because of, ourselves. This same Ishmael has been the driving force—sometimes intentional, often subliminal—behind Del Tredici's artistic vision for more than thirty years. Del Tredici's approach, like Ishmael's, is that of the engaged observer who directly addresses viewers using common elements in uncommon ways, alerting us loud and clear to what we but vaguely intuit, and in the process finding his way to our very core.

I ought to know. In my classroom, Del Tredici's work has been a sea change for my students, from honors high-schoolers to university graduates. His bold Melville imagery has time and again jolted viewers into awareness of their own soundings and of the deeper resonances of universal myth.

I favor a hands-on approach. With humpback whale songs as background (by Larkin, by Paul Winter/Paul Halley/Leonard Nimoy), I invite students to wander the teaching space at will and gaze on Del Tredici's framed *Moby-Dick* illustrations lining the perimeter of the room, to take in the twelve-foot scroll along one wall and the slides I project continuously onto another. Students select the image that most "speaks" to them, bringing it back to their desk or gathering near the scroll or slide projector to ponder . . . and write.

Discussions the next day are mercurial. The illustrations often act on students like tarot cards, triggering surprising combinations of meaning with different arrays. The "cave-art" quality of Del Tredici's pictures and the primal colors of the paper stock draw viewers in. Strong framing and jittery cross-hatching evoke mental states that are insistent and gutsy. Melville's roisterous wisdom comes shining through student commentary on many levels.

Meditation and Water (Chapter I) ignites the most discussion (see Plate 4). "Water is where we can be cleansed," says one student, "freeing ourselves from anger." Another ventures, "This picture tells me the sea is holy, something to be worshipped, a truth to be found in *Moby-Dick*, though I'm not

sure I'm able to look at it." Another thoughtfully offers, "This pen-and-ink is truly awesome. The more I think about it, the more it connects with me. It is about trying to approach God."

Whiteness of Whale, where "subtlety appeals to subtlety, and without imagination no man can follow another into these halls" (Chapter XLII), shows a diminutive Ishmael gliding in the slipstream of a majestic cetaecean (see Plate 53). Students are abuzz over this image, flagging its contrasts in perspective and perception, noting tensions between knowledge and chaos, equanimity and terror.

Grand Contested (Chapter I) is "so NOW," enthuses one student (see Plate 8). "Ishmael's walking on the water's very edge near those pointy shark-fins. I've been there, too!" I feel "kicked in the stomach," says another, face-to-face with *Lazarus and Dives* (Chapter II), who explains, "My life has been a happy little bubble; Mr. Del Tredici's suffering Lazarus made me wonder: What if my entire world crumbled?" (see Plate 15).

Del Tredici's illustration *Hyena* (Chapter XLIX) captures an eldritch energy that sneaks up and bites us where the sun doesn't shine—a wild jester presence mocking our cosmic cluelessness (see Plate 26). It moved one student to reflect that God is "not a cruel taskmaster but a comic puppeteer. We should laugh at ourselves in the midst of being embarrassed."

God's Foot (Chapter XCIII), says a student, "shows us Pip's brush with a higher power. It's all muscle, something that could crush him like a bug. Do you think Pip's levitation changed the molecules in his body?" (see Plate 29).

Though Del Tredici's graphic approach is unique, even idiosyncratic, he did not work in a vacuum. Most significantly, he knew and loved the art of Rockwell Kent (1882–1971). Kent had ridden the crest of the Melvillean renaissance and spent four years illustrating *Moby-Dick* (first published in 1930 and continuously reprinted), producing more images for Melville's epic than any other American illustrator. His pen-and-ink drawings act as headpieces and tailpieces to the chapters and throughout the text as scenes that track the novel's narrative development. Kent's maritime experiences around Newfoundland, Alaska, Chile, and Greenland provided him with enduring images of mountain gorges, stormy swells, great vessels, and pelagic life. His firmly controlled linework delivers charged images of languor and ferment, with regal whales that strike poses ranging from ponderous and playful to vacant and profound. Kent's strongest human character is Ahab, a man he often depicts with tortured intensity. But his treatment of seer-narrator Ishmael is infrequent and lacks acuity.

Del Tredici pored over Kent's edition of *Moby-Dick* during the 1960s while working on his own pen-and-ink drawings for the novel. He was most struck by the atmospherics of Kent's india-ink drawings, which he felt captured "an eerie cosmic wholesomeness." But the great majority of Kent's illustrations hewed to the epic's narrative structure so thoroughly that Del Tredici felt no need to pursue that dimension. Kent freed Del Tredici to take a more metaphysical tack, exploring Ishmael's boisterous humor and far-ranging, free-spirited philosophical musings instead of the shipbound, ill-fated narrative that absorbed Kent and has spellbound most Melville illustrators before and since.

I often compare parallel *Moby-Dick* images by Kent and Del Tredici to highlight these artists' differing sense of Melville's vision. One depicts Queequeg in a whaleboat at night: "There, then, he sat, holding up that imbecile candle in the heart of that almighty forlornness. There, then, he sat, the sign and symbol of a man without faith, hopelessly holding up hope in the midst of despair" (Chapter XLVIII). Kent's presentation is upbeat, almost serene. This mariner seems to be praying, and, though his boat needs bailing and his head hangs low, the lantern on the end of his pole decisively disperses the midnight gloom.

Del Tredici intentionally modeled his "candle" illustration on Kent's as an homage. But while he appropriates the structure of Kent's design, Del Tredici transforms it to express Queequeg's despondency, alienation, and briny existential angst. Queequeg's scalpknot becomes a gangly tuft that floats with eerie languor while his shoulders hunch and cower. Absent from the image are swamped boat and crew. What we have here is a one-on-one encounter between savage and cosmos, with no happy ending in sight. Del Tredici has replaced Kent's cheery shafts of light with guttering rays from a truly "imbecile" candle that wanly awaits extinction. As one student observed, "Here is a situation where hope just isn't practical. Queequeg will be swallowed by the darkness." This picture has proven to be a magnet for my young adult students, grappling as they

The First Lowering (Chapter XLVIII), Rockwell Kent.
Courtesy of the Plattsburgh State Art Museum, Rockwell Kent Collection.

Imbecile Candle, Robert Del Tredici.

must with parental expectations not always receptive to their own unformed, unexpressed, though no less ardently felt, aspirations.

In Kent's final Epilogue image, Ishmael appears to be undergoing a resurrection as he rises from his briny ordeal on Queequeg's coffin. Neck thrown back, he lifts one arm skyward with opened palm, his face rapt in the expectation of mercy and grace; the heavens above stream down benediction in canticles of light.

Del Tredici's Epilogue image, his newest pen-and-ink design, done in early 2000 and based on his experiences swimming in the Caribbean Gulf Stream, projects Ishmael's doubt outward from Ishmael to the horizon and inward to the very roots of the narrator's stranded soul. There are no prayers or blessings here; we find instead salt-encrusted locks of hair, sunburned cheeks, and a gaze that has survived Ahab's tasking and heaping only to become transfixed by the void. A shark's muscular fin brushes Ishmael's thigh. The sea-hawk's shadow falls like Fate between the man, his past (the "closing vortex" of a sunken *Pequod*), and his fragile future—dimly discerned as the "devious-cruising *Rachel*."

Kent's final Ishmael suggests apotheosis; it could almost be seen as a form of liturgical art. Kent was profoundly moved by Melville, but he was evidently not shattered by Melville's vision. Del Tredici's final Ishmael gives us point-blank

Epilogue, Rockwell Kent. *Courtesy of the Plattsburgh State Art Museum, Rockwell Kent Collection.*

Bimini Ishmael, Robert Del Tredici.

open-endedness, black holes, and a contemplative interior vision that does not deliver us from evil.

Melville's spiritual quest did not end with *Moby-Dick*. It extended the following year to *Pierre*, where the protagonist falls into ambiguities so vertiginous that suicide is the only exit. It continued for two decades more to *Clarel*, where a pilgrimage to the Holy Land offers no deliverance. At Melville's death, the tension was still taut between his recognition of salvific potential and his heart's inability to realize it. Like a haruspex, Del Tredici examines Ishmael's entrails and divines a haunted/hunted pain that glints with tentative openness at the wide ambivalent world of the Great Spirit.

Until now, my students and I have entered the tortured, buoyant world of Del Tredici's *Moby-Dick* illustrations through their original black-and-white designs. Thirty years later, these designs are emerging from Del Tredici's silkscreen studio clothed in coats of radiant colors that bring to life, perhaps for the first time, the invisible palette of Melville's own cosmic tints. Though Melville could not have guessed the precise hues and glints of these shimmering postmodern expressions, Del Tredici's vision captures bone-deep Melville's own relentless joy and ineluctable ambiguity.

Flood Tide

Del Tredici's Return to Printmaking

ROBERT K. WALLACE

Like many members of the rapidly expanding audience for Robert Del Tredici's *Moby-Dick*-inspired artworks, I first came to know them through Elizabeth Schultz's 1995 book *Unpainted to the Last*.[1] Even in the radically reduced size imposed by the format of the sheltering, nurturing, birthing book, in which the original 8½" x 11" prints from the 1960s were reproduced as 2¾" x 3¾" figures, Del Tredici's remarkable images came through loud and clear. As Schultz's text so quickly helped us to see, here was a new, quirky, canny vision of *Moby-Dick*. With a unique knack for exploring diverse dimensions of Ishmael's quicksilver narrative, Del Tredici's mesmerizing images slipped seamlessly from the comedic to the horrific, quickening our response to the words from the novel that the artist had lettered into his respective working spaces.

How wonderful it was for me and my students at Northern Kentucky University, in a course on Melville and the Arts during the 1996 spring semester, to be able to read Schultz's newly published book immediately after reading *Moby-Dick*. Even better was it to be able to see Schultz's exhibition "Unpainted to the Last" at Northwestern University after having savored her book of the same name.[2] We had been initiated into Del Tredici's graphic style and literary acuity during Brian Cruey's classroom presentation from Schultz's book, but our appreciation intensified when Brian stood before the full-sized prints in Evanston and brought out even more of their visual punch and conceptual zing.

1. Elizabeth Schultz, *Unpainted to the Last:* Moby-Dick *and Twentieth-Century American Art* (Lawrence: U of Kansas P, 1995), figs. 8.38–55, pp. 210–28.

2. The exhibition "Unpainted to the Last" had opened at the Spencer Art Museum at the University of Kansas in Lawrence in August 1995. After a stop at the University of Michigan in Ann Arbor, it completed its travels at the Mary and Leigh Block Gallery at Northwestern University in Evanston, Illinois (Jan. 12–Mar. 3, 1996).

Our augmented joy in the presence of the prints themselves turned out to be a precursor to those new sensations that Del Tredici has more recently evoked when, after being brought back to Melville by Schultz's book, he began to transform those youthful pen-and-inks into the spacious, gestural, iridescent screenprints featured here in *Floodgates of the Wonderworld*.

My students and I had the pleasure of meeting Del Tredici when we returned to Illinois in April 1997 for our "Landlocked Gam," a joint exhibition of *Moby-Dick* art with students of Rockford College at the Rockford College Art Gallery.[3] Del Tredici was one of four professional artists whom the students invited to exhibit with them, and he chose to display six experimental screenprint enlargements he had made in the 1970s. As a keynote speaker, he opened his illustrated lecture with an account of how wrestling with Melville had helped him keep his head above water in the wake of his disillusionment as a seminary student. He then recounted the vagaries of fate that had led him to become a photographer of Orson Wells, Hyman Rickover, and the Cold War nuclear weapons industry during a thirty-year period in which he had nominally left Melville behind.

When I next taught a course in Melville and the Arts during the 1998 spring semester, our Honors Program invited Del Tredici to campus as our Conference of Honors speaker. I curated an exhibition of his *Moby-Dick* prints and nuclear photographs to coincide with the Honors presentation and the last half of my course.[4] This group of students, after assimilating *Moby-Dick*

and *Unpainted to the Last,* plunged into two books of Del Tredici's nuclear photography. Like their 1996–97 predecessors, these students decided at the end of the semester to mount an exhibition of their own *Moby-Dick* art; Del Tredici's graphic influence was in some cases as visible as Melville's literary influence.

Del Tredici's versatility and vitality as a campus visitor led to his being invited to return to Highland Heights in May 1999 to teach a course in the history of animated film. By now he was obsessed with creating a new kind of screenprint from his earlier *Moby-Dick* designs, especially as he had been invited to give a plenary address at an international conference on "Melville and the Sea" at Mystic Seaport that June. A printmaker on our campus provided him access to her studio for the duration of his stay. There, in the evenings, he transformed himself from a savvy photographer who stalks and shoots reality into a rejuvenated printmaker who creates and recreates graphic worlds. Del Tredici needed help during his three-week crash-course in advanced screenprinting and found it in two of my former *Moby-Dick* students who served as his lab assistants, Aaron Zlatkin and Ellen Bayer.[5] I had the

3. "Landlocked Gam: *Moby-Dick* Art by Students at Rockford College, Northern Kentucky University, and Guest Artists: Vali Myers, Frank Stella, Robert Del Tredici," Rockford College Art Gallery, Rockford, Illinois, Apr. 7–25, 1997.

4. "Whales, Atoms, Eyes: The Art of Robert Del Tredici," Exhibition, Fine Arts Foyer, Northern Kentucky University, Highland Heights, Kentucky, Apr.–May 1998.

5. For Zlatkin's and Bayer's account of their opportuni-

pleasure of witnessing the new kind of expression that came into being as Del Tredici swiped glittering pigments onto the poster-sized sheets with increasing gestural vigor, using each porous screen as an agent of transformation as well as replication.

Del Tredici had hoped to produce a suite of new screenprints for the Mystic conference, but the work became more demanding than he anticipated. I watched him work on the print that signaled a sea change in his approach. After he had built up an increasingly expressive combination of undercolors on the successive sheets of *Sick Civilized,* Del Tredici applied the decisive "hit" that was to complete the image: overlaying the black contours of his original line drawing. Rather than resolving the image, however, these bold black lines now seemed to imprison it. Del Tredici halted the press run after four prints while he took in the implications of this unexpected crisis. At Mystic he displayed the unfinished abstract version of *Sick Civilized* alongside its "imprisoned" companion, keeping his options open.

My first glimpse of his resolution to this impasse came in April 2000, when Elizabeth Schultz arrived on our campus as that year's Conference of Honors speaker. At a welcoming party for Schultz, Ellen Bayer, who had assisted

Del Tredici the previous May, showed the dazzling new screenprint of *God's Foot,* fresh from the studio in Montreal (see Plate 29). In it Del Tredici had transformed black cross-hatchings into spun-gold filaments. In another bold stroke, he reversed the values in God's foot, printing it as a negative image. This manipulation of design elements was a breakthrough. He had cut loose from the tyranny of the original pen-and-ink structure.

My next chance to chart the evolution of his screenprinting technique came in July 2000. The Kent State University Press had expressed interest in publishing *Floodgates of the Wonderworld.* Del Tredici, Elizabeth Schultz, Jill Gidmark, and I met at Arrowhead, the house in Pittsfield, Massachusetts, where Melville lived and wrote. We came together to brainstorm about the book. As Del Tredici lifted one new print after another from his portfolio, we saw how he was evolving light years from where he had started just a year before.

In their introductory comments, Schultz and Gidmark call attention to the otherworldly, iridescent tints of *God's Foot* and to the Gulf Stream magic of *Bimini Ishmael.* I would like to look at the scarred, gorgeous, transformative surface of *Left Wing Day of Judgment* (see Plate 45). The visceral inspiration for the original pen-and-ink drawing was Ishmael's vision of the black smoke from the whale whose body is burning in "The Try-Works." In enlarging the image to screenprint size, Del Tredici might well have intensified the black coloration of the drawing. Instead, he suffused the entire image with fiery

---

ties to associate with Del Tredici in increasingly responsible roles, see his "Coffins into Life Buoys" and her "Straight from the Whale's Mouth," companion essays to my "Opening those Flood-Gates of the Wonder-World," in "On Teaching Melville," a special issue of *Leviathan* 2 (Oct. 2000): 33–53.

orange. This is not the orange of seething flame but rather the scathing, psychic residue of conscious choices made by mankind in relation to the physical and spiritual worlds that surround our kind. I find this luminous millennial print more frightening than its pen-and-ink original—and more beautiful, too, especially in the incongruous beauty of the colors screened into the area of the sheet imprinted with the words, colors whose smooth hues deepen the cross-hatched lacerations surrounding the whale and its smoke. These lacerations are already present, to be sure, in the black lines of the original drawing, but those are not as dark, true, or wounding as these bright, quick strikes in burnt-orange.

How can such incongruous colors and whiplash lacerations work so well in a print inspired by the blackness of darkness? I suppose by what they reveal of the artist's exquisite control of his medium, of the unconscious creative joy that results from embodying, effectively, even the grimmest of truths. In this bright print we feel the full force of Ishmael's impassioned wish: "Would that he consumed his own smoke! for his smoke is horrible to inhale, and inhale it you must, and not only that, but you must live in it for the time" (Chapter xcvi).

A few days after we had arrived in Pittsfield, Frank Stella came up to see Arrowhead. Stella had completed his *Moby-Dick* series in 1997, creating one or more artworks for every chapter title of the novel. He was now planning for a summer 2001 exhibition of his abstract prints and industrial sculptures at Arrowhead to celebrate

Homage to Stella, Robert Del Tredici.

the 150th anniversary of the publication of *Moby-Dick*. Stella met Del Tredici and looked at some of his most recent screenprints. When he saw the first one he asked, "How do you get those effects?" The conversation that followed over the picnic table at Arrowhead was to have a lasting effect on Del Tredici's approach to printmaking.

Del Tredici had already been thinking of Stella when making silkscreens at Northern Kentucky University in May 1999. Stella's influence was implicit in the abstract gestural border of *Inscrutable Tides of God* (see Plate 23) and explicit in *Homage to Stella,* an impromptu collage that Del Tredici composed in the studio with by-products of the printmaking process. The abstract juxtapositions of color and form in this 1999 collage anticipated the increasingly abstract fluidity of the prints *God's Foot, Left Wing,* and *Bimini Ishmael* he was to bring to Arrowhead a year later. The augmented abstraction of these prints was to intensify further in such post-Arrowhead prints as *Ahab's Glare, Grand Contested, Boggy Soggy,* and *Ahab: Mountain Wave,* each of which moves Del Tredici farther from the initial aesthetic of pen-and-ink drawings tightly tied to a text. He attributes this visual intensification to the "torch of graphic mischief" that he felt Stella had passed on to him in their Arrowhead encounter. Del Tredici was not yet ready to "go whole hog abstract," and he was "still keeping the narrative element" of his original drawings, but he was now allowing the narrative thread to "spin and dangle by thinner and thinner filaments."[6] Peering into the mountain wave with Ahab in the frontispiece of this book, we ride the flood tide of a narrative artist who has internalized the text of *Moby-Dick* so deeply as to trust entirely the wonder of his own graphic vision.

Stella and Del Tredici converge on *Moby-Dick* from opposite directions, but they have become increasingly close in artistic approach. Stella has been an abstract artist from the time of his Black Paintings of 1958–60, whereas Del Tredici has been a narrative and figurative artist in his pen-and-ink illustrations of 1964–66. But Stella's abstract art became more narrative and figurative during his work on the *Moby-Dick* series (1985–97), just as Del Tredici's illustrative art became more abstract in his screenprint fabulations of

1999–2001.[7] Melville had himself moved from a figurative aesthetic toward a more abstract one in the process of writing *Moby-Dick,* achieving one of his finest and most characteristic balances between the two in Ishmael's depiction of the squitchy picture in the Spouter-Inn. Pictorial artists who respond most deeply to Ishmael's vision often find themselves, before they are done, as did Melville himself, oscillating between the figurative and the abstract in the drift and the drive of their own expressive needs.

6. Robert Del Tredici, letter to the author, Oct. 23, 2000.
7. Stella's stylistic transformation is discussed at length in my *Frank Stella's* Moby-Dick: *Words and Shapes* (Ann Arbor: U of Michigan P, 2000).

THE PLATES

Plate 1: *Cracked about the Head.* Pen & ink, 1964.

Herman
Melville
1819 – 1891

Heaven have mercy on us
all — Presbyterians and Pagans
alike — for we are all
somehow dreadfully cracked
about the head, and sadly
need mending.

(Moby-Dick, ch. XVII)

Plate 2: *The Flea*. Pen & ink, 1964.

NO GREAT AND ENDURING VOLUME CAN EVER BE WRITTEN ON THE FLEA, THOUGH MANY THERE BE WHO HAVE TRIED IT. (Ch. CIV)

Plate 3: *Great Whale.* Pen & ink, 1964.

Chief among my motives was the overwhelming idea of the great whale himself.

Plate 4: *Meditation and Water*. Pen & ink, 1966.

Yes, as every
one knows,
meditation and water
are wedded
forever.

Plate 5: *Narcissus.* Pen & ink, 1965.

Still deeper the meaning of that story of Narcissus, who because he could not grasp the tormenting, mild image he saw in the fountain, plunged into it and was drowned. But that same image, we ourselves see in all rivers and oceans. It is the image of the ungraspable phantom of life; and this is the key to it all. (Ch.I)

Plate 6: *Knocking Hats Off*. Pen & ink, 1964.

Plate 7: *Floodgates of the Wonderworld.* Original pen & ink, 1965. Silkscreen print, 2001.

The great flood-gates of the wonder-world swung open, and in the wild conceits that swayed me to my purpose, two and two there floated into my inmost soul, endless processions of the whale, and, mid most of them all, one grand hooded phantom, like a snow hill in the air.

(Ch. I Loomings)

Plate 8: *Grand Contested.* Original pen & ink, 1964. Silkscreen print, 2000

Plate 9: *Barbarous Coasts.* Original pen & ink, 1959, 1964. Digitally worked.

With other men, perhaps, such things would not have been inducements; but as for me, I am tormented with an everlasting itch for things remote. I love to sail forbidden seas, and land on barbarous coasts. Ch I

Plate 10: *Congregation of Ants.* Original pen & ink, 1966.

I cherish the greatest respect towards everybody's religious obligations, never mind how comical, and could not find it in my heart to undervalue even a congregation of ants worshipping a toadstool.

ch. XVII:
The Ramadan

Plate II: *Faith Like a Jackal.* Pen & ink, 1965.

Plate 12: *Boggy Soggy.* Original pen & ink, 1965, 1999. Silkscreen print, 2001

A boggy, soggy, squitchy picture truly, enough to drive a nervous man distracted.

Plate 13: *Abominable Tumblers.* Original pen & ink, 1966. Silkscreen print, 2001.

ABOMINABLE are the TUMBLERS into which he POURS his POISON.

(Ch III *The Spouter-Inn*)
©1966 BDT

Plate 14: *Quick Chaotic*. Pen & ink, 1965.

Yes, there is death in this business of whaling—
a speechlessly quick chaotic bundling of a man
into Eternity. But what then? Methinks we have
hugely mistaken this matter of Life and Death. (ch VII)

©1965 BDT

Plate 15: *Lazarus and Dives*. Pen & ink, 1965.

Now, that Lazarus should lie stranded there on the curbstone before the door of Dives, this is more wonderful than that an iceberg should be moored to one of the Moluccas. (ch. II)

Plate 16: *Stave My Soul.* Pen & ink, 1966.

Methinks that what they call my shadow here on earth is my true substance. Methinks that in looking at things spiritual we are too much like oysters observing the sun through the water, and thinking that thick water the thinnest of air. Methinks my body is but the lees of my better being. In fact take my body who will, take it I say, it is not me. And therefore three cheers for Nantucket; and come a stove boat and a stove body when they will, for stave my soul, Jove himself cannot.

Methinks that what they call my shadow here on earth is my true substance. Methinks that in looking at things spiritual we are too much like oysters observing the sun through the water, and thinking that thick water the thinnest of air. Methinks my body is but the lees of my better being. In fact take my body who will, take it I say, it is not me. And therefore three cheers for Nantucket; and come a stove boat and a stove body when they will, for stave my soul, Jove himself cannot.

(CH.VIII The Chapel) ©1966 BDT

Plate 17: *Cannibal Springs.* Pen & ink, 1965.

The next moment the Light was extinguished, and this wild cannibal, tomahawk between his teeth, sprang into bed with me.

(Ch. III: The Spouter-Inn)

© 1965 BDT

Plate 18: *Apple Dumpling.* Pen & ink, 1964.

Plate 19: *Intolerable Allegory*. Original pen & ink, 1965. Silkscreen print, 2001

So ignorant are most landsmen of some of the plainest and most palpable wonders of the world, that without some hints touching the plain facts, historical and otherwise, of the fishery, they might scout at Moby Dick as a monstrous fable, or still worse and more detestable, a hideous and intolerable allegory.

So ignorant are most landsmen of some of the plainest & most palpable wonders of the world, that without some hints touching the plain facts, historical and otherwise, of the fishery, they might scout at Moby Dick as a monstrous fable, or still worse and more detestable, a hideous and intolerable allegory.

Plate 20: *Immortal Species.* Pen & ink, 1964. Digitally worked.

$\mathfrak{W}$herefore, for all these things, we account the whale immortal in his species, however perishable in his individuality.

He swam the seas before the continents broke water;

he once swam over the site of the Tuileries, and Windsor Castle, and the Kremlin.

In Noah's flood, he despised Noah's Ark; and if ever the world is to be again flooded, like the Netherlands, to kill off the rats, then the eternal whale will survive, and rearing upon the topmost crest of the equatorial flood, spout his frothed defiance to the skies.

CI
Does the Whale's Magnitude Diminish—
Will He Perish?

Plate 21: *As with a Bird.* Pen & ink, 1966.

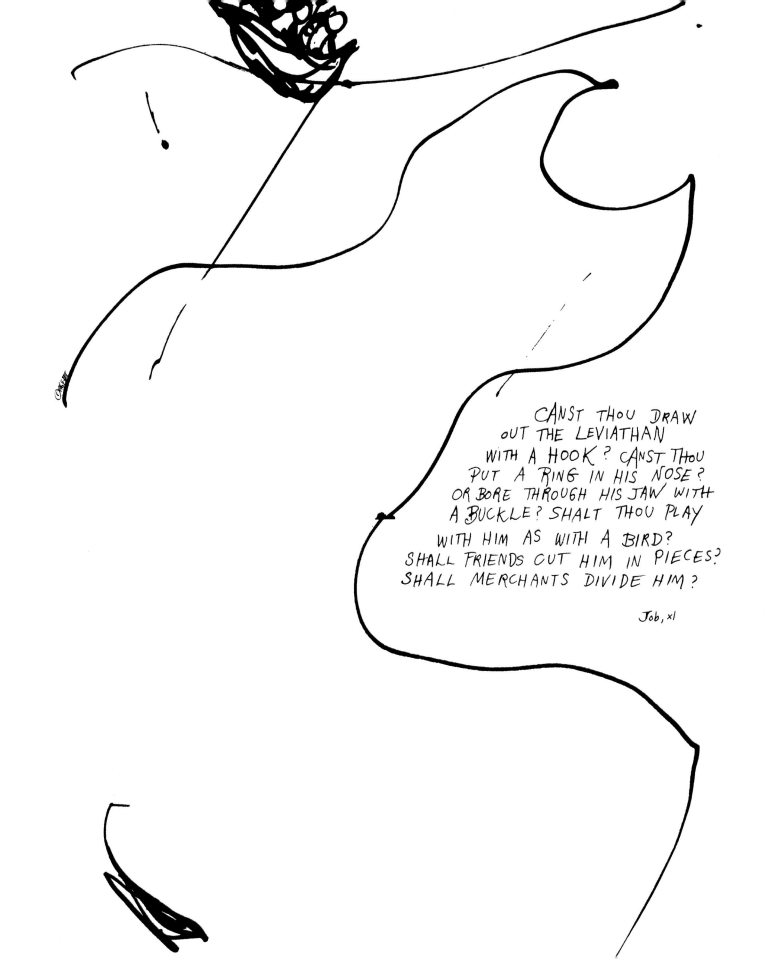

CANST THOU DRAW
OUT THE LEVIATHAN
WITH A HOOK? CANST THOU
PUT A RING IN HIS NOSE?
OR BORE THROUGH HIS JAW WITH
A BUCKLE? SHALT THOU PLAY

WITH HIM AS WITH A BIRD?
SHALL FRIENDS CUT HIM IN PIECES?
SHALL MERCHANTS DIVIDE HIM?

Job, xl

Plate 22: *Insular Tahiti*. Pen & ink, 1965.

CONSIDER them both, the sea and the land; and do you not find a strange analogy to something in yourself? For as this appalling ocean surrounds the verdant land, so in the soul of man there lies one insular Tahiti, full of peace and joy, but encompassed by all the horrors of the half known life. God keep thee! Push not off from that isle, thou canst never return!

[Ch. LVII]

©1965 BDT

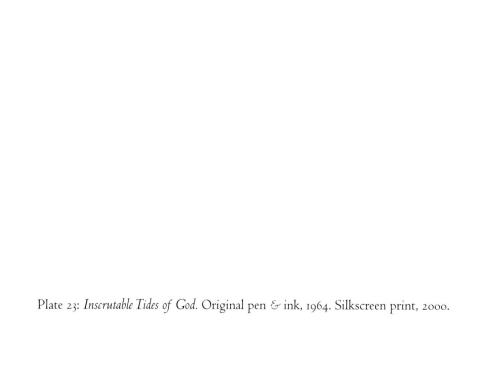

Plate 23: *Inscrutable Tides of God.* Original pen & ink, 1964. Silkscreen print, 2000.

Plate 24: *Ahab Stands Alone.* Pen & ink, 1964.

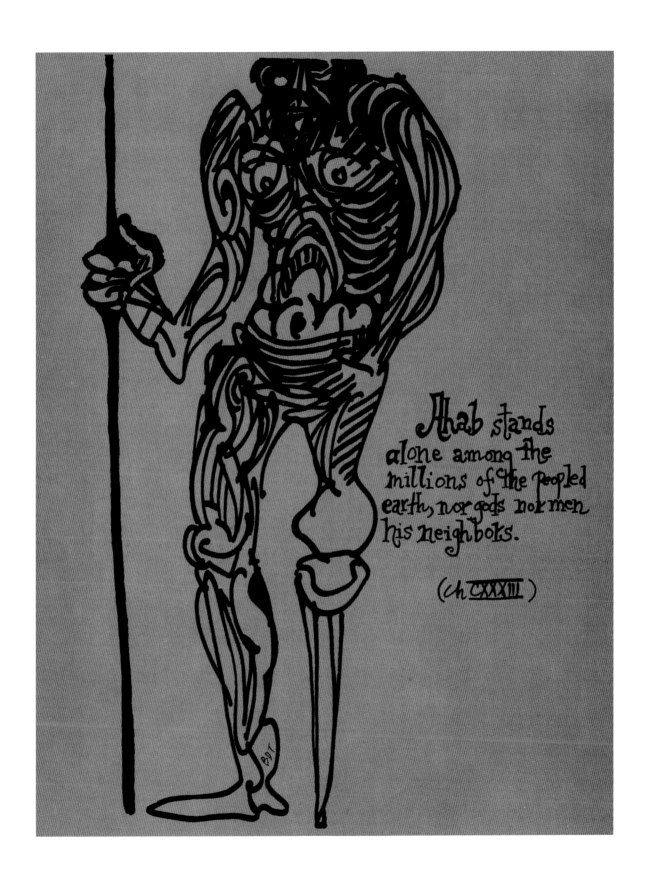

Ahab stands alone among the millions of the peopled earth, nor gods nor men his neighbors.

(ch CXXXIII)

Plate 25: *Queequeg and His Mark.* Pen & ink, 1964.

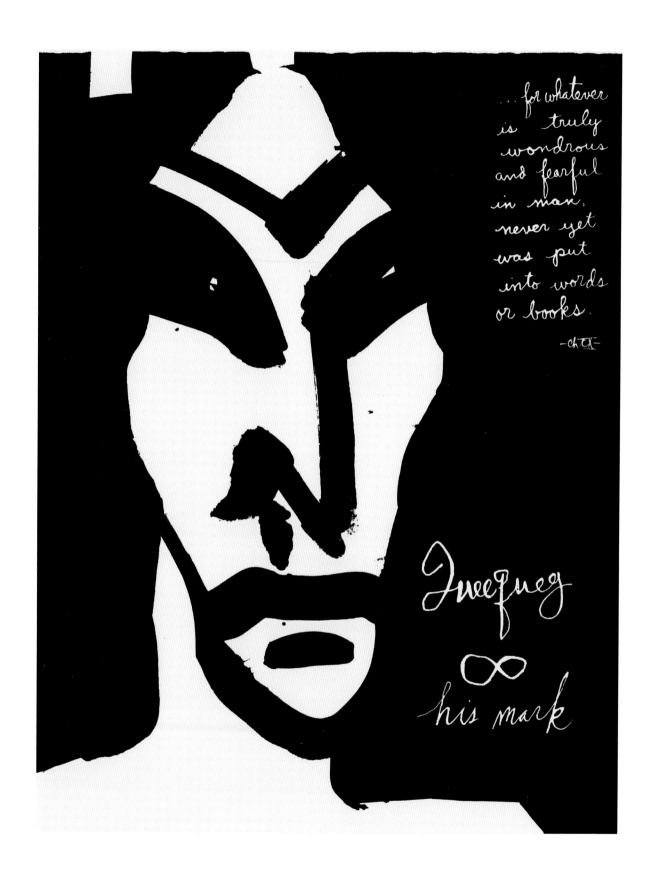

...for whatever is truly wondrous and fearful in man, never yet was put into words or books.

—Ch. CX—

Queequeg

∞

his mark

Plate 26: *Hyena.* Pen & ink, 1965.

There are certain queer times and occasions in this strange mixed affair we call life when a man takes this whole universe for a vast practical joke, though the wit thereof he but dimly discerns. (Ch. XLIX the Hyena)

Plate 27: *Kingdom of Cetology.* Pen & ink, 1965.

I am aware that down to the present time, the fish styled Lamatins and Dugongs (Pig-fish and Sow-fish of the Coffins of Nantucket) are included by many naturalists among the whales. But as these pig-fish are a nosy, contemptible set, mostly lurking in the mouths of rivers, and feeding on wet hay, and especially as they do not spout, I deny their credentials as whales, and have presented them with their passports to quit the Kingdom of Cetology.

(Ch. XXXII: Cetology) ©1965 BDT

Plate 28: *Ahab: Mountain Wave.* Original pen & ink, 1966, 2000. Silkscreen print, 2000.

Plate 29: *God's Foot.* Original pen & ink, 1964. Silkscreen print, 1999.

Carried down alive to wondrous depths, Pip saw God's foot upon the treadle of the loom, and spoke it; and therefore his shipmates called him mad.

Ch. XCIII "Castaway"
©1967 BOX

Plate 30: *Ahab's Tools.* Pen & ink, 1964.

To accomplish his object

Ahab must use tools, and of all tools used in the shadow of the moon,

MEN are most apt to get out of order.

©1964 BDT

Plate 31: *Starbuck.* Pen & ink, 1966.

Horrible old
man!
Who's above him,
he cries;—aye, he
would be a democrat to
all above; look, how
he lords it over all below!
Oh!
I plainly see my miserable
office to obey, rebelling;
and worse yet,
to hate with touch of pity.

Starbuck

Plate 32: *Ahab Glare.* Original pen & ink, 1966. Silkscreen print, 2001

. . . there lurked a something in the old man's eyes, which it was hardly sufferable for feeble souls to see.

...there lurked a something in the old man's eyes, which it was hardly sufferable for feeble souls to see.

Plate 33: *Sun-dried Ears.* Pen & ink, 1965.

With greedy ears I learned the history of that murderous monster against whom I and all the others had taken our oaths of violence and revenge.

(Ch. XLI) ©Aes BPT

Plate 34: *Mortal Heedful.* Pen & ink, 1965.

The weaver-god, he weaves; and by that weaving is he deafened; and by that humming, we, too, who look on the loom are deafened; and only when we escape it shall we hear the thousand voices that speak through it. For even so it is in all material factories.

The spoken words that are inaudible among the flying spindles; those same words are plainly heard without the walls, bursting from the opened casements. Thereby have villainies been detected. Ah, mortal! then, be heedful; for so, in all this din of the great world's loom, thy subtlest thinkings may be overheard afar. A Bower in the Arsacides

Plate 35: *Wild Watery.* Pen & ink, 1965.

Plate 36: *Seat Thyself Sultanically.* Pen & ink, 1965.

Seat thyself sultanically among the moons of Saturn, and take high abstracted man alone; and he seems a wonder, a grandeur, and a woe.

ch. XVII The Carpenter
©1965 BOT

89

Plate 37: *Celebrate a Tail.* Pen & ink, 1965. Digitally worked.

Other poets have warbled the praises of the soft eye of the antelope, and the lovely plumage of the bird that never alights; less celestial, I celebrate a tail.

(CH. LXXXVI: The Tail)

Plate 38: *Sick Civilized.* Original pen & ink, 1966. Silkscreen print, 1998, 2000.

Now, there is this noteworthy difference between savage and civilized; that while a sick, civilized man may be six months convalescing, generally speaking, a sick savage is almost half-well again in a day.

IX Queequeg in his Coffin ©melger

Plate 39: *Charmed Churned Circle.* Pen & ink, 1965.

Not the raw recruit, marching from the bosom of his wife into the fever heat of his first battle; not the dead man's ghost encountering the first un- -known phantom in the other world; —neither of these can feel stranger and stronger emotions than that man does, who for the first time finds him- self pulling into the charmed, churned circle of the hunted sperm whale.

(Ch. XLVIII: The 1st Lowering)

© AG5 BOT

95

Plate 40: *Imbecile Candle.* Pen & ink, 1965.

There, then, he sat,
holding up that imbecile
candle in the heart of
that almighty forlornness.

There, then, he sat,
the sign and symbol of a
man without faith,
hopelessly holding up hope
in the midst of despair.

Ch. XLVIII
The First Lowering
©1965 BDT

Plate 41: *Hist.* Pen & ink, 1966.

Plate 42: *Gods Not Glad.* Pen & ink, 1965.

To trail the genealogies of these high mortal miseries carries us at last among the sourceless primogenitures of the gods; so that, in the face of all the glad, hay-making suns, and soft-cymballing, round harvest moons, we must needs give in to this: that the gods themselves are not for ever glad.

The ineffaceable, sad birthmark on the brow of man, is but the stamp of sorrow in the signers.

Ch. CVI
Ahab's Leg

©BDT 1965

Plate 43. *Ahab's Cards.* Original pen & ink, 1965. Digitally worked.

Plate 44: *Careful Disorderliness.* Original pen & ink, 1965. Silkscreen print, 2000.

There are some enterprises in which a careful disorderliness is the true method. LXXII

Plate 45: *Left Wing Day of Judgment.* Original pen & ink, 1964. Silkscreen print, 2000.

The smoke of the whale has an unspeakable, wild, Hindoo odor about it, such as may lurk in the vicinity of funereal pyres. It smells like the Left Wing of the day of judgment; it is an argument for the pit.

Ch XCVI

Plate 46: *Iron Crown of Lombardy.* Pen & ink, 1965.

Is, then, the crown too heavy that I wear?
this Iron Crown of Lombardy. Yet is it bright with
many a gem; I, the wearer, see not its far
flashings; but darkly feel I wear that, that
dazzlingly confounds.

XXXVII ©1965 BDT

109

Plate 47: *Mutual Joint Stock World.* Silkscreen print, 1965.

Was there ever such unconsciousness?
He did not seem to think that he at all
deserved a medal from the Humane
and Magnanimous Societies.
He only asked for water - fresh water -
something to wipe the brine off.

Mildly eyeing those around him,
he seemed to be saying to himself —
"It's a mutual, joint-stock world, in all meridians.
           We cannibals must help these Christians."

Plate 48: *Royal Mantle*. Pen & ink with color offset ink, 1966.

But this august dignity I treat of, is not the dignity of kings and robes, but that abounding dignity which has no robed investiture.

Thou shalt see it shining in the arm that wields a pick or drives a spike;

that democratic dignity which, on all hands, radiates without end from God! Himself! The great God absolute! The center and circumference of all democracy! His omnipresence our divine equality!

If, then, to meanest mariners, and renegades and castaways, I shall hereafter ascribe high qualities, though dark; weave round them tragic graces; if even the most mournful, perchance the most abased among them all,

shall at times lift himself to the exalted mounts; if I shall ever touch that workman's arm with some ethereal light; if I shall spread a rainbow over his disastrous set of sun;

Then against all mortal critics bear me out in it, thou just Spirit of Equality, which hast spread one royal mantle of humanity over all my kind!

©1956 BDT

XXXVI Knights & Squires

Plate 49: *Folly Beast of Earth.* Original pen & ink, 1966. Silkscreen print, 1998.

Plate 50: *Mystical Brow*. Original pen & ink, 1966. Silkscreen print, 2001.

Human or animal,
the mystical brow is as that great golden seal
affixed by the German Emperors to their decrees.
It signifies—God: done this day by my hand.

LXXIX

Plate 51: *Pasteboard Masks.* Original pen & ink, 1966. Silkscreen print, 2001.

All visible objects, man, are but as pasteboard masks. But in each event — in the living act, the undoubted deed — there, some unknown but still reasoning thing puts forth the mouldings of its features from behind the unreasoning mask. If man will strike,

strike through the mask! How can the prisoner reach outside except by thrusting through the wall? To me, the white whale is that wall.

© 1966 BbT

XXXVI: The Quarter-Deck

Plate 52: *Bullet Train Whale.* Pen & ink, 1966.

To me the white whale is that wall, shoved near to me. Sometimes I think there's naught beyond. But 'tis enough. He tasks me; he heaps me. I see in him outrageous strength with an inscrutable malice sinewing it. That inscrutable thing is chiefly what I hate.

—Ahab XXXVI QuarterDeck

©66 BDT

Plate 53: *Whiteness of Whale.* Pen & ink, 1965.

In a matter like this,
subtlety appeals to subtlety,
and without imagination
no man can follow another
into these halls.

The Whiteness of the Whale
XLII

© 1965 BDT

123

Plate 54: *Equal Eye.* Original pen & ink, 1966. Silkscreen print, 2000.

Doubts of all things
earthly, and
intuitions of some
things heavenly;

this combination
makes neither
believer nor infidel,
but makes a man
who regards both
with equal eye.

Plate 55: *Undiscovered Prime.* Pen & ink, 1965.

And, AS FOR ME, IF, BY ANY POSSIBILITY, THERE BE ANY AS YET UNDISCOVERED PRIME THING IN ME; IF I SHALL EVER DESERVE ANY REAL REPUTE IN THAT SMALL BUT HIGH HUSHED WORLD WHICH I MIGHT NOT BE UNREASONABLY AMBITIOUS OF; ...IF, AT MY DEATH, MY EXECUTORS, OR MORE PROPERLY MY CREDITORS, FIND ANY PRECIOUS M.S.S. IN MY DESK, THEN HERE I PROSPECTIVELY ASCRIBE ALL THE HONOR AND THE GLORY TO WHALING; FOR A WHALE-SHIP WAS MY YALE COLLEGE AND MY HARVARD. (Ch XXIV)

Plate 56: *Worming Undulation.* Pen & ink, 1965.

My hypothesis is this: that the spout of the whale is nothing but mist. To this conclusion I am impelled by considerations touching the great inherent dignity and sublimity of the Sperm Whale. I account him no common, shallow being, inasmuch as it is an undisputed fact that he is never found on soundings, or near shores; all other whales sometimes are. He is both ponderous and profound. And I am convinced that from the heads of all ponderous, profound beings, such as Plato, Pyrrho, the Devil, Jupiter, Dante, and so on, there always goes up a certain semi-visible steam while in the act of thinking deep thoughts.

While composing a little treatise on Eternity, I had the curiosity to place a mirror before me. and ere long saw reflected there, a curious involved worming and undulation in the air over my head. The invariable moisture of my hair, while plunged in deep thought, after six cups of tea in my thin shingled attic, of an August noon; this seems an additional argument for the above supposition.

(Ch. LXXXV: The Fountain)

Plate 57: *Methusaleh.* Pen & ink, 1970. Digitally worked.

Plate 58: *Bimini Ishmael*. Original pen & ink, 1965, 1998, 2000. Silkscreen print, 2000.

Buoyed up by that coffin, for almost one whole day and night, I floated on a soft and dirge-like main. The unharming sharks, they glided by as if with padlocks on their mouths; the savage sea-hawks sailed with sheathed beaks. On the second day, a sail drew near, nearer, and picked me up at last. It was the devious-cruising Rachel, that in her retracing search after her missing children, only found another orphan.

Buoyed up by that coffin, for almost one whole day and night, I floated on a soft and dirge-like main. The unharming sharks, they glided by as if with padlocks on their mouths; the savage sea-hawks sailed with sheathed beaks. On the second day, a sail drew near, nearer, and picked me up at last. It was the devious-cruising Rachel, that in her retracing search after her missing children, only found another orphan.

EPILOGUE © BDT 2000

133

Plate 59: *Face in Water*. Original pen & ink, 1965. Silkscreen print, 2000.

Herman Melville, 1855. Courtesy of Corbis/Bettmann.

Cracked About the Head, pen-and-ink portrait of Herman Melville based on the Corbis/Bettmann photograph, 1964.

Postscript

ROBERT DEL TREDICI

Herman Melville saved my life. He shed boisterous new light on the ancient wisdom that we are irrevocably damaged—without invoking Original Sin or seeking Salvation. His insight and restraint freed up in me a mass of compacted energy that self-ignited and went on to burn like rocket fuel.

That energy had been solidifying in me over an eight-year period inside a Roman Catholic seminary in California. I attended St. Joseph's and St. Patrick's minor and major Sulpician seminaries in fulfillment of a childhood dream to become a priest. We studied hard, all the time, Latin and Greek, poetry and rhetoric, *The Imitation of Christ, Lives of the Saints*. We played team sports, sang Gregorian chant, staged Gilbert and Sullivan, renounced thoughts of females, took vows of silence, confessed sins on Fridays, and continually pondered the state of our souls.

Within those hallowed walls, I developed a proclivity for cartooning that found expression in posters, stage sets, the school newspaper, philosophy notes, and a covert freelance greeting card operation based on bright ideas from a cadre of brainstorming friends. My designs were picked up by Rex Cards, a small studio in San Francisco that silk-screened greeting cards by hand and distributed them nationally. During vacations I'd visit the shop to admire the ingenuity of this ancient printmaking technology harnessed to such worldly ends.

My initiation into the mysteries of the hierarchy of the Church was cut short at age twenty-two. After finishing two-thirds of the twelve-year program, I was assailed by doubts—and riddled with certainties—about my place, or lack of it, in the ecclesiastical scheme of things. I staggered out of the institution a ruined soul and gravitated toward the only activity I could connect with: more study.

At the University of California, Berkeley, I took philosophy then literature. Alain Renoir

Rex greeting card #25-503. Pen-and-ink drawing transferred to silkscreen, January 1959.

spotted my classical background and gave me my first-ever job as a teaching assistant for a freshman section of comparative lit. I couldn't resist illustrating passages from the required readings, cranking out purple mimeographed sheets to *Don Quixote, Crime and Punishment, Notes from the Underground,* and *The Prince.* Working up imagery for this band of schemers, misfits, ax-murderers, and errant do-gooders proved sound foundation for what lay in store with the next book on the list, *Moby-Dick.*

I'd not read Melville before. "Loomings" electrified me. Its narrator hit closer to home, struck deeper, got darker, and was idiosyncratically more hilarious than any other fictional character I'd met. I felt compelled to illustrate this phenomenal tale and upgraded my means of

production from purple mimeograph to quill-and-ink, getting the drawings reproduced on colored stock at a local offset print shop.

The picture that kick-started the series had narrator Ishmael, on emerald paper, clenching his fists and glaring at pedestrians under the words, "Whenever . . . it requires a strong moral principle to prevent me from deliberately stepping into the street and methodically knocking people's hats off—then I account it high time to get to sea as soon as I can."

Ishmael's state reflected my own, and his penchant for articulating brutal truths in droll terms made him seem familiar, like family. But this clever talker was more than the sum of his sound bites. Here was a man with a mission—though at first he had no clue as to what that

ROBERT DEL TREDICI

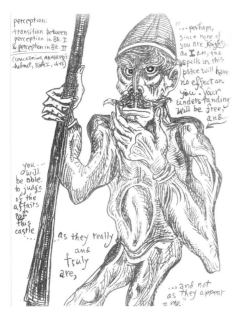

Illustration to Don Quixote, by Miguel de Cervantes Saavedra. Mimeographed drawing, September 1963.

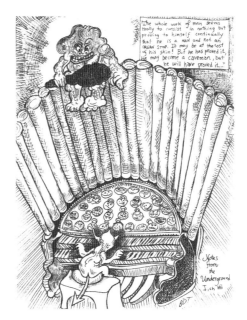

Illustration to Notes from the Underground, by Fyodor Dostoevsky. Mimeographed drawing, November 1963.

mission was. He goes to sea, in fact, to sidestep self-destruction. Once embarked, Ishmael does not pursue whales or vengeance as much as his own native independence, embracing the chaotic preconditions for knowledge and pondering time and again the dynamics of perception. I bonded right off with this character whose knack for mirroring me back to myself kept me suspended in amazement.

There was more: Ishmael's eccentric celebration of the human condition encouraged me to peer through my own fissures into a world more luminous and ambivalent than I ever would have guessed. The heartfelt sweep and precision of his insights gave me confidence to move like a co-conspirator into a universe where cetaceans abounded, infernal hyenas made stunning

appearances, and Ahab's poisoned soul commandeered the landscape. Through it all Ishmael's spirit flew hoops around Captain and crew and soared into the heart of the cosmos. It dawned on me early that Melville was no conventional teller of tales; he had crafted here a crinkly, sprawling blueprint for surviving any journey I might imagine, especially the one I felt in my bones I was on—a journey shot through with abandonment, promising to end in vertigo on an open sea, fried by cosmic rays, food for sharks.

Poet David Schooley was a student in my freshman section. A loner, he sized me up as if he were contemplating pitching a golden spear through my chest. He liked my illustrations and showed me some of his poems. I was stunned.

Urubamba

The sadness of tremendous mountains
weeps from the jagged faces of a lost race.
Indian lips wail through pipes of reed and bone
and red crystals splash out of focus
in the grey gullies of an ancient night
where winds drunk with altitude
carry the bleeding roar of the conch
and muddy lakes swell across the sky
thundering on the misty shores of the moon.
A race of silent prophets, whipped and damned,
digs for roots in the dripping terraced hills,
for the bread of famine and the wine of thirst.
An unbegotten people, shadows on the mighty rock,
dance to the fluttering tears of a flute.

David was the first person I met who was a
living link to Melville. His appetite for the wild
edge of things combined with an understanding
of the subtle ways of evil to make him a boon
companion. When he offered to take me down to
Yucatan one winter break, I jumped at the chance
and brought *Moby-Dick* along for good luck. In
the poet's company, Mexico's sinister, sweet clime
put me outside my known universe. I had
glimpses that the world might be partly my own
idea, that its prime matter lay just beneath the
surface, and the potential for sustenance, synapse,
and betrayal lay everywhere.

Back in Berkeley I finished my degree. People
were still recovering from the Kennedy
assassination; the university community was split
by the Free Speech Movement, opposed to
Vietnam, energized by Dylan's "Blowin' in the
Wind," and increasingly entranced by New Age

drugs. Berkeley also had America's first repertory
cinema, where, in lieu of knocking hats off or
killing whales, I sat through multiple screenings
of films by Bergman and Kurosawa.

In the spring I completed my MA thesis, a
probe into the art of book illustration called
"Illustrated in Wonderland: A Century of
Illustrations to *Alice's Adventures in Wonderland*." As
far as I could tell, only two artists had
successfully combined image with text for this
book, the first being Lewis Carroll, whose
amateur sketches inspired the splendid
realizations of Punch cartoonist Sir John Tenniel.
These two men had enhanced the spirit of the
story while remaining faithful to its words.
Illustrators after them fell short on both counts.

Bowery Mendicant, New York City, May 1, 1978.

ROBERT DEL TREDICI

Orson Welles at Boston Symphony Hall, ca. 1977.

he declared it empty of spirit and full of addiction.

Through it all I kept on with the Melvilles, each new visualization driving a stake through the heart of my turmoil. I felt I could keep illustrating this book forever; but two non-events drew my work on the series to a close. An editor at Northwestern University Press had wanted to incorporate fifty of my designs into an edition of *Moby-Dick*; he kept the illustrations for a year before returning them with regrets. Also, I was driving a motorcycle at this time and was having more than my share of close calls. So in an effort to sidestep self-termination, I vowed to trade in my artistic ambition for a teaching job wherever I might find one. I found one in an alien land, in a city I'd not heard of, bought a used VW van, spray-painted it metallic green, and set a course north by northwest for Mount Royal Junior College in Calgary, Alberta, Canada, feeling more like Queequeg in his coffin than Ishmael on the decks of any *Pequod*.

With this crossing I put *Moby-Dick* behind me. But four years of immersion in its mercurial waters had quickened my instincts with energies that seemed to realign my chromosomes. The book had kept my religious instincts tingling in the void, made the void itself a familiar realm, kept my feet pointed outward, and caused the absence of a safety net to propel me into action. It had also managed to shed penetrating light into that vacuum-sealed vault for meaning buried deep inside my brain.

For three years I taught courses in English, humanities, and cinema. I'd relinquished my

I then put academia behind me and began to make my way as an artist, doing landscape drawings, paintings, more *Moby-Dick* pen-and-inks, and some silkscreen printing—all the while delivering mail, working in a can factory, shucking oysters, and teaching part time at a free school.

These became my wandering years. I got enmeshed with con men, outcasts, gurus, and communes as I traveled the California coast, camped on top of Half-Dome, hopped freights to Arizona, and spent nine months in Spain on a Fulbright. I settled in San Francisco during the dark finale of the hippie era. Zap Comix had just hit the streets, and Fillmore Rock posters set the aesthetic. George Harrison and Patty visited the Haight-Ashbury district while I was living there;

dream of becoming an artist so was caught off guard when my image-making energies surged back the moment I picked up a 35 mm camera. In a heartbeat photography became my new medium. Not nearly so jealous a mistress as drawing, it was perfectly suited to a fragmented lifestyle. I started with street photography, moved to Montreal to teach film history, began a series of portraits of film makers, and in 1978 took a leave to study photography and film in Manhattan.

While I was living in New York, the meltdown at Three Mile Island occurred. It put Middletown, Pennsylvania, on the world map. The stricken reactor was 200 miles from my doorstep. I knew nothing about commercial nuclear power stations but felt an urge to make portraits of the southeastern Pennsylvania "natives" who had lived through this unprecedented event. For one year I rode trains into the region and, with camera and tape recorder, tracked the accident's aftermath. My wanderings through towns and valleys around the crippled reactor crystallized in me a vision of misty radiation releases, institutional lies, and a deep, lambent, unnameable havoc. *The People of Three Mile Island* became my first book in 1980.

The early 1980s saw Europe enraged at NATO for siting cruise and Pershing missiles on its soil. Dr. Helen Caldecott responded in the U.S. by electrifying the collective imagination with visions of nuclear fireballs over modern cities; and Jonathan Schell weighed in with *The Fate of the Earth,* his sustained meditation on humanity's

Middletown Housewife Joyce Corradi opposes the venting of radioactive Krypton-85 gas into her community as part of the cleanup of the damaged Three Mile Island reactor. NRC Public Meeting, Liberty Fire Hall, Middletown, Pennsylvania, March 19, 1980.

nuclear self-extinction. I hated to admit it, but the jig seemed up: any day now we'd be getting what we deserved—a mutually assured atomic inferno on our heads. But the apocalypse hadn't befallen yet, and the thought occurred to me that perhaps I might do something in the meantime.

I decided to go after the H-bomb factories. Everywhere people were wringing their hands over the prospect of atomic mushrooms blooming overhead, but nobody mentioned the plants that were churning out three to six new warheads daily. If one slightly used reactor could

ROBERT DEL TREDICI

Model of the Uranium Atom. Uranium is the basic element from which nuclear explosives are made. Museum of Science and Energy, Oak Ridge, Tennessee, June 11, 1982.

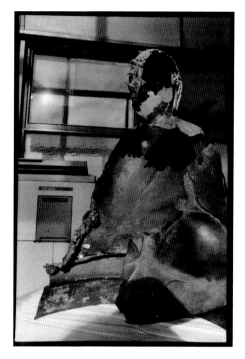

Hiroshima Buddha. This bronze statue was melted by heat from the Hiroshima bomb. Hiroshima Peace Museum, Japan, November 13, 1984.

turn peoples' lives inside out the way Three Mile Island had done, what, I wondered, must life be like in the shadow of those older, darker reactors that for thirty years had been making plutonium for bombs? It wasn't the Bomb's explosive glory that drew me in; I was captured by our resolute mass production of nuclear weapons and the impact this had to be having on the bodies and souls of everyone involved.

But I was not yet up to knocking on bomb factory doors, so I went to Hiroshima and Nagasaki to learn the human meaning of a nuclear weapon. Aging survivors did not hold back; they knew that I could have no idea of what

it's like to experience the atom bomb. When I told them my plan to photograph the bomb factories, they said what I needed to hear: "Yes, you must do this."

It took six years. I started with overflights, visited towns and cities near the plants, and met with public relations personnel whose mission was to interface with members of the press. My suppressed ecclesiastical training stirred when I realized I was facing yet another hierarchy supporting yet another unseen omnipotent creator-destroyer with legions of anointed devotees. Knowing the language of hierarchy helped me get inside five of the twelve major

The Becquerel Reindeer. Radioactive reindeer contaminated by fallout from Chernobyl, stored in a slaughterhouse locker at Harads Same-Produktor, Harads, Lapland, Sweden, December 3, 1986.

All the Warheads in the U.S. Nuclear Arsenal. This installation, entitled "Amber Waves of Grain" by artist Barbara Donachy, contains 25,000 miniature ceramic nose cones. Boston Science Museum, February 13, 1985.

plants that make up the American H-bomb complex. I crisscrossed the United States three times; journeyed through Canada's uranium fields; photographed reactors and nuclear reprocessing plants in England, France, and Germany; and, right after Chernobyl, photographed a frozen heap of radioactive reindeer in Swedish Lapland.

I called my second book *At Work in the Fields of the Bomb.* When I finished it, I surprised myself with the notion of documenting that secret-within-a-secret, the Soviet Bomb. I mailed my new book to Gorbachev in care of the Kremlin, got no reply, made my way to Moscow twice to test the waters, raised interest but no action from Mir Publishers, and ended up inside the system soon after the empire collapsed in 1991.

I was a third of the way through the former-Soviet project when two brushes with death in

Russia, one of them medical and the other mechanical, made me back off and reconsider—this just as Hazel O'Leary was designated Clinton's secretary of Energy. Her signature issue was openness throughout the bomb complex, and she hired key people to make it happen. One of them was Jim Werner, whom I'd met on my last Russian trip. He invited me to help him highlight the need to clean up the American bomb plants. Most of the U.S. factories, by now well beyond their design life, had been shut down for temporary safety fixes, which, one after the other, turned into permanent closures. The radioactive contamination that these plants had been steeped in became for the first time a focus of attention as Energy shifted its mission from weapons production to cleanup. Sensing a unique opportunity, I joined forces with the Energy Department in a race against time to revisit the

American bomb plants "from headquarters" before they were demolished. I helped Jim Werner design three official reports on the present, past, and future of cleanup activities at the weapons sites. Most government reports have as their subtext "Trust us." My mission was to make sure the images in these documents put a face on the system that would awaken viewers to the gritty reality and low-key terror of the situation.

For nearly two decades I probed the Bomb's secrecy, its cultural invisibility, the elusiveness of its radiation, the numbing enormity of its infrastructure, and the banality of its long-lasting wastes with their hidden threat to land and bone and blood and mind and spirit. These were areas of concern that, in retrospect, I saw reflecting a Melvillean perspective. I felt no conscious link to Melville during my nuclear travels, but more than once the thought occurred to me that Melville would not have been surprised to learn about the Bomb. From the day Los Alamos physicists called the first one by its code name "The Gadget" to the epoch of the world's superpower arsenals, the author of *Moby-Dick* would, I imagined, have taken in our nuclear age with a rock-steady gaze. I didn't have to prove this beyond reflecting on Melville's insight into human need and folly, his sense of humanity's embryonic conscience and its genocidal streak, and his grasp of monomania with its zest for annihilation.

Yuliy B. Khariton at age eighty-eight. Along with Zeldovich and Sakharov, Khariton was a principal developer of the Soviet H-bomb. Stalin made Khariton director of Arzamas-16, the first Soviet nuclear weapons laboratory. Khariton, thrice declared a "Hero of Soviet Labor" by Stalin, ran the lab for forty-eight years. Moscow, May 20, 1992.

Maids of Muslyumovo. Tartar-Bakshir women watch Americans measure radiation in the Techa River where it flows past their town. For four years during the 1940s, Soviets poured high-level nuclear waste into the Techa in their haste to catch up with the U.S. bomb program. Villagers downstream were not informed. Muslyumovo, Chelyabinsk region, Russia, May 23, 1992.

Drums of Transuranic Waste contaminated with plutonium sit on a concrete pad in temporary storage. Plutonium has a half-life of 24,400 years. E Area Burial Grounds, Savannah River Site, South Carolina, January 7, 1994.

I was also convinced that Melville would not have missed a beat on hearing of the CIA, crimes against humanity, species extinction, black holes, or used car salesmen. His way of viewing life from the brink, through a lens darkly, not assuming happy endings, not yielding to despair, helped me a hundred and fifty years afterward to better navigate my own late great American century. Melville's descriptions of the American whale fishery of the 1840s and 1850s turn out to be the best account we have of that industry's workings, yet his observations had such interiority that they shed more precious light on the dynamics of the human psyche. His approach guided me toward grappling with the nuclear weapons industry as a metaphor for consciousness.

I do not know of any other writer like Melville, whose syntax is so shot through with cosmic tints, whose spirit ignites such reader collaboration. When I picked up the leviathan's shining trail again after thirty-odd years of other pursuits, the energy of *Moby-Dick* lay waiting for me, perfectly undimmed, as if freed from a time capsule. It straightaway returned me to my roots in art, taking me beyond black-and-white into a universe of color. Silkscreens rushed in where pen-and-ink once tread to abet me in the trapping of the play of Melville's mind, and "careful disorderliness" became indeed "true method" for once more breaking through the book's narrative crust into that blend of mind and matter embedded like marrow in its text.

Robert Del Tredici, Northern Kentucky University print-making studio, May, 1999. *Photograph by Robert K. Wallace.*